The Best of Grimm's Fairy Tales

Containing:

The Best of Grimm's Fairy Tales

Illustrated by Svend Otto S

*Translated by Anthea Bell
and Anne Rogers*

Larousse & Co., Inc.

This edition first published in the USA by
Larousse & Co. Inc.,
572 Fifth Avenue,
New York NY 10036,
1979

First published in Denmark by
Gyldendal
1979

Puss in Boots and *Tom Thumb* translated by
Anthea Bell, *Snow White and the Seven
Dwarfs*, *The Wolf and the Seven Little Kids*
and *The Musicians of Bremen* translated by
Anne Rogers from *Kinder und Hausmarchen*
(1812)

ISBN 0-88332-150-5 (trade edition)
      0-88332-122-X (library edition)

Library of Congress Catalog Card
No.: 79–63439

Printed in Denmark

Snow White
and the Seven Dwarfs

It was midwinter and snow was falling like feathers. A young Queen sat by the window to do her embroidery, which she kept flat in an ebony frame. As she looked up from her work to watch the snow, she pricked her finger and three drops of blood fell on the snow on the window-ledge. She looked at the little patch of red on the snow and thought: "I'd love to have a child as white as snow, as red as blood and with hair as black as this ebony frame."

After a while she did indeed have a baby daughter as white as snow, as red as blood, and with hair as black as ebony, so she called her Snow White. Soon after her child was born the young Queen died.

A year went by and the King married again. His new Queen was beautiful, but she was proud and stony-hearted. She was so vain that she couldn't bear to think that anyone else might be more beautiful than she. She often looked in her magic mirror and asked:

"Mirror, mirror on the wall,
Who is the fairest of us all?"

And the mirror answered:

"O Queen, you are the fairest in the land."

Then the proud Queen was satisfied, for she knew that the magic mirror spoke nothing but the truth.

But as time went by Snow White became even more beautiful. When she was seven she was as lovely as a sunny day and far lovelier than the Queen herself. One morning when the Queen went to her mirror and asked:

"Mirror, mirror on the wall,
Who is the fairest of us all?"

the mirror replied:

"O Queen, yours is a beauty rare,
But Snow White is a thousand times more fair."

The Queen was horrified and turned yellow and green with jealousy. From that moment whenever she saw Snow White her blood ran cold with hatred.

Soon afterwards she sent for a huntsman and said:

"Take the child out into the forest; I can't bear the sight of her. Kill her, and bring me her liver as proof – I'll reward you well."

The huntsman took Snow White into the forest and was about to plunge his knife into her innocent heart, but she begged him:

"Please spare my life, dear huntsman; I'll run into the forest and never come back, I promise you."

The huntsman couldn't bring himself to harm her and said:

"There, then, run along, you poor child."

He thought of the wild animals in the forest and believed she would not live long.

At that moment a young wild boar bounded into sight so he killed it and removed its liver to take to the Queen as proof that her wicked instructions had been obeyed.

Now poor Snow White was all alone in the forest, trembling with fear. She began to run. Wild birds and beasts scuttled past her but did her no harm. She ran until she could run no further. By then it was almost dark, but she could just see a little house. She went up to it to ask for shelter, but nobody was at home.

She went in to rest for a while. Everything in it was very small but beautifully clean and tidy. Snow White was amazed to see a round table laid ready for seven, with a knife, fork and spoon and a glass of wine beside each plate. Against the wall were seven neatly made little beds.

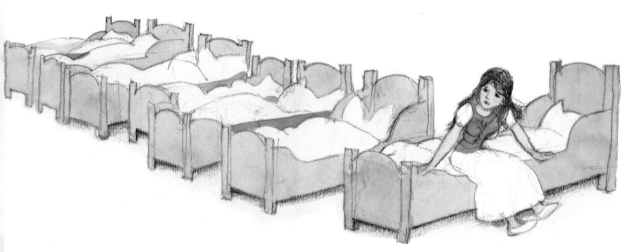

Snow White was so hungry and thirsty that she ate a mouthful of food from each plate and drank a sip of wine from each glass. (She thought it would be unfair to take everything from one person's place.) By now she was ready to lie down, for she was very tired. She tried each bed in turn; the first was too long for her, the next was too short, but when she came to the seventh bed it was just right, so she settled down and fell fast asleep.

When it was quite dark the masters of the house came home. They were seven dwarfs, and they had been working all day digging for gold in the mountains. They lit their lanterns and soon saw that someone had been in the house while they were out.

The first said: "Who's been sitting on my chair?"

The second said: "Who's been eating from my plate?"

The third said: "Who's taken a bite from my bread?"

The fourth said: "Who's had some of my cabbage?"

The fifth said: "Who's used my fork?"

The sixth said: "Who's used my knife?"

"Who's been drinking from my glass?" said the seventh.

The first dwarf looked round and noticed a dent in his pillow. "Who's been lying in my bed?" he asked, and the others ran to their own beds and exclaimed: "Mine too!"

When the seventh dwarf looked at his bed, he discovered Snow White, fast asleep. He called the others and they all gasped when they saw the lovely girl lying there.

"Heavens! What a beautiful child!" they whispered. They were so delighted to see her sleeping so peacefully that they didn't wake her up. The seventh dwarf slept with one of his brothers, an hour with each in turn, until morning.

When Snow White woke up she saw the seven dwarfs. At first she was frightened, but she soon found that they were gentle and friendly.

"Who are you?" they asked her.

"My name is Snow White," she said.

"How did you find our house?" they asked.

So Snow White told them that the huntsman had taken her to the forest on the orders of her stepmother who wanted to get rid of her, but he had spared her life.

The dwarfs said: "If you'll help with housework and keep things clean and tidy for us, you may stay here, and we'll take good care of you."

"Oh, thank you!" said Snow White. "I will gladly do all I can to help you; I'd love to live here with you."

So she stayed with the seven dwarfs and they were all very happy. When they got home each evening Snow White had a good supper ready for them. As she was on her own all day long, the kind dwarfs warned her:

"Beware of your stepmother; she may know where you are by now, so don't let anyone in."

But the wicked Queen had had proof, as she thought, of Snow White's
death. So when she asked her mirror:

"Mirror, mirror on the wall,
Who is the fairest of us all?"

she could hardly believe the answer:

"O Queen, yours is a beauty rare,
But Snow White's a thousand times more fair.
With seven dwarfs she's living now,
The loveliest lady still, I vow."

The Queen's blood ran cold, for she knew that the mirror spoke nothing
but the truth. She realized that the huntsman had lied to her and had not
killed Snow White after all. She was determined to get rid of the girl. At
last her plan was ready. She stained her face brown and disguised herself
as an old pedlar woman, so that she was quite unrecognizable. She found
out where the seven dwarfs lived and set off over the hills. Soon she came
to the house and knocked on the door, calling out:

"Fine ribbons for sale! Best quality laces!" Snow White looked out of the window and said:

"Good afternoon. What are you selling, please?"

"Fine ribbons, fair maid, best quality laces," the old woman replied, holding up a pretty ribbon of pure silk.

"I'm sure it will be all right to let this poor old woman in," thought Snow White. She unbolted the door and bought the silk ribbon for her bodice.

"Just let me show you how to tie it properly," said the crafty Queen.

Quite unsuspecting, Snow White allowed the old woman to thread the ribbon through her bodice. Quick as lightning, she laced it so tightly that Snow White couldn't breathe and fell down as though dead. The old woman hurried away.

Soon afterwards the seven dwarfs finished their day's work and came home. They were horrified to find Snow White lying on the floor, apparently dead. Gently lifting her up, they saw that she was much too tightly laced, so they cut the silk ribbon to free her. Snow White began to breathe again, and soon sat up and was able to talk. When the dwarfs heard what had happened, they said:

"That old woman must have been the wicked Queen in disguise. Do be careful. You must never again let anyone in when we're not here."

The Queen had reached home by now. She ran to her magic mirror and asked eagerly:

"Mirror, mirror on the wall,
Who is the fairest of us all?"

But to her fury the mirror replied, as before:

"O Queen, yours is a beauty rare,
But Snow White's a thousand times more fair.
With seven dwarfs she's living now,
The loveliest lady still, I vow."

When the Queen heard this, her blood froze with rage, for she realized that Snow White must have recovered.

"Next time there will be no mistake," she muttered.

Using a witch's evil spell, she made a poisoned comb. Again she disguised herself as a pedlar, set off over the hills, knocked at Snow White's door and called:

"Fine ribbons for sale! Best quality brushes and combs!"

Snow White looked out and said nervously:

"I'm not allowed to let anyone in. And I don't need anything today, thank you."

"I won't come in, then," said the old woman. "But just look at this golden comb – you'd like that, wouldn't you?" She held out the glittering comb and at once Snow White fell under its spell and longed to have it. She unbolted the door and bought the comb. The old woman said:

"Now just let me comb your pretty hair, my beauty."

Still suspecting nothing, Snow White let the old woman have her way. As soon as the comb touched her hair, the poison began its deadly work and the girl again fell lifeless to the ground. The old woman hurried away.

By now night was falling and the dwarfs were on their way home. When they found Snow White unconscious, they knew that her wicked step-mother had been in the house again. They searched Snow White and soon found the poisoned comb. When they removed it from her hair, Snow White recovered and explained what had happened. So they again urged her never to let anyone in if they were not there.

Back at home, the Queen ran to her room and asked:
    "Mirror, mirror on the wall,
    Who is the fairest of us all?"
And yet again the mirror replied:
    "O Queen, yours is a beauty rare,
    But Snow White's a thousand times more fair.
    With seven dwarfs she's living now,
    The loveliest lady still, I vow."
At this the wicked Queen shook with rage.

    "Right!" she said. "This time I'll find a way to finish her off once and
for all."

    She went to a secret cellar and made a deadly poisonous apple. It looked
harmless enough, but whoever took a bite would fall down dead at once.

When the fatal apple was ready, the wicked Queen again disguised herself as a peasant, set off over the hills and knocked at the dwarfs' door. Snow White called through the window:

"I can't let anyone in – I've promised not to."

"I quite understand," said the old woman. "But my apples are very heavy and I'm trying to get rid of them. Look, I'll give you this lovely rosy one."

"No, thank you," said Snow White. "I'm not allowed to take it."

"Are you afraid of being poisoned?" asked the crafty Queen. "Well, look – I'll cut the apple in two. You can eat the red half and I'll eat the rest."

The juicy apple was very skilfully made, and only the red half was poisoned. Snow White's mouth watered as she looked at it. When she watched the old woman eating the green half, she could not resist the offer of the red half. She took a bite – and fell down dead.

The wicked Queen laughed aloud at her success.

"White as snow, red as blood and black as ebony!" she jeered. "The dwarfs won't save you this time."

She rushed home to ask, as before:

> "Mirror, mirror on the wall,
> Who is the fairest of us all?"

And at last the mirror gave the answer she wanted:

> "O Queen, you are the fairest in the land."

And now the Queen's heart was content – that is, so far as an envious heart can ever be content.

When the dwarfs came home they found Snow White lying dead on the floor. They lifted her up and looked closely to see how she could have been poisoned again, but found nothing. They loosened her bodice, combed her hair and washed her in water and wine, but it was no use. Unable to revive her, they feared that she was dead.

They laid her in a glass coffin and carried it to the mountain top, and there they wept over her for three days, each taking it in turn to keep guard. They put her name on the coffin in golden letters, saying that she was a King's daughter. Animals and birds came to the mountain and mourned with them – first an owl, then a raven, then a dove.

But they could not believe Snow White was really dead. She was still white as snow, red as blood, and her hair as black as ebony. She seemed to be asleep, so they went on hoping that one day she would wake up again.

One evening a young prince was riding in the forest. He came to the

dwarfs' home and asked to spend the night there. He saw the glass coffin on the mountain, and gazed in wonder at the lovely girl lying as though asleep. He read her name and stayed watching her for a long time. Then he said to the dwarfs: "Let me have the coffin, and I will pay whatever you ask." But the dwarfs replied:

"We wouldn't part with it for all the gold in the world."

So the prince said:

"Then I beg you to give it to me. I can't live without Snow White. I will love her and look after her for ever."

He spoke so tenderly that the dwarfs had pity on him and gave him the coffin. As the prince and his servants were carrying it down the mountain, one of them stumbled over a low bush and jerked the coffin. The sudden jolt loosened the piece of poisoned apple, and it fell from Snow White's mouth. Very soon she opened her eyes, lifted the coffin lid and sat up.

"Oh! – where am I?" she said.

"You're with me, Snow White," replied the prince. He told her what had happened, and how he had found her.

"I love you more than words can say. Come home with me to my father's castle. You shall be my wife."

Snow White fell in love with the prince and gladly went home with him and agreed to marry him. The seven dwarfs were invited to the wedding, and so was Snow White's stepmother. The wicked Queen put on her finest clothes and once more asked her usual question:

"Mirror, mirror on the wall,
Who is the fairest of us all?"

And this time the mirror answered:

"O Queen, yours is a beauty rare,
But the bride, Snow White, is a thousand times more fair."

At this the jealous Queen flew into such a violent rage that she fell down dead. Nobody was sorry.

Snow White and the prince were married with great pomp and splendour and lived happily ever after.

The Wolf and the Seven Little Kids

Once upon a time there was a mother goat. She had seven little kids and she loved them all very dearly. One day she wanted to go to the wood to find food, so she called all her family and said:

"I'm going to the wood, my dears. Don't let the wolf come in—if he gets in here he'll gobble you up. He is cunning and he may try to disguise himself, but you'll know him by his gruff voice and his black feet."

"We'll be very careful, Mother," said the little
kids. "Don't worry. We shall be quite all right while
you're away." So their mother said goodbye and
trotted away happily.

Soon afterwards there was a knock on the door
and a voice called out:

"Open the door, my dears! It's your mother. I've
brought you each a present."

But the little kids could tell by his gruff voice that
it was the wolf.

"We won't open the door," they said. "Our
mother has a sweet and gentle voice, but your voice
is gruff. You're the wolf!"

The wolf ran off to a shop and bought a big piece of chalk. To make his voice soft he swallowed the chalk. Then he went back to the house, knocked on the door and called out:

"Open the door, my dears! It's your mother. I've brought you each a present."

But the wolf's black paw was on the window-sill.
When the little kids saw it they said:

"We won't open the door. Our mother hasn't got
black feet like you. You're the wolf!"

So the wolf ran off to a baker and said:

"I've hurt my foot. Put some dough on it." The baker did so. Then the wolf went to a miller and said: "Put some white flour on my foot."

The miller refused, for he thought: "The wolf

wants to trick someone." But the wolf said:

"If you don't do as I tell you, I'll eat you up!"
The miller was frightened, so he made the wolf's
foot white with flour. Yes, people do behave like
that sometimes.

The wicked wolf went to the house for the third time, knocked on the door and said:

"Open the door, my dears! It's your mother. I've come back home and I've brought you each a present."

The little kids called out:

"First show us your foot so that we can see if you are really our mother."

So the wolf put his paw on the window-sill, and when the little kids saw the foot was white, they believed what they had been told and opened the door. But it was not their mother who came in. It was the wolf!

The little kids were terrified and tried to hide.

The first dived under the table,

the second burrowed
under the bedclothes,

the third jumped into the oven,

the fourth dashed into the kitchen,

the fifth into the cupboard,

the sixth under
the wash-tub, and

the seventh climbed into
the grandfather clock.

But the wolf found six of the little kids and swallowed them in six great gulps.

He couldn't find the youngest, who was still hiding in the clock.

Feeling fat and full, the wolf staggered off to the nearest field, lay down under a tree and fell fast asleep.

Soon the mother goat came home from the wood. What a sight met her eyes! She found the door wide open, table and chairs overturned, crockery smashed and bedclothes pulled off the bed. She looked everywhere for her children, but where were they? She couldn't find any of them.

She called them each by name, but there was no answer. Then, when she called the name of her youngest, a little voice answered: "Here I am, Mother. I'm in the clock."

She lifted him out and he told her that the wolf had eaten up all the rest. How the mother goat cried! After a while the goat and her little one trotted

out into the field. There they saw the wolf lying
sound asleep under the tree, snoring so loudly that
the leaves shook and shivered. The mother goat
carefully examined the wolf from every angle. She
could see something wriggling inside his stomach.

"Heavens!" she thought. "My poor children! Can they still be alive, even though the wolf swallowed them for supper?"

She sent her youngest running to the house for scissors, needle and thread.

She began to cut open the wolf's stomach. One of the little kids popped his head out. She cut the skin a bit more, and one after the other her six children jumped out. They were still alive, and had come to no harm. The wolf was so greedy that he'd swallowed them whole.

How happy they were again now! They hugged and kissed their mother and skipped for joy.

"Go and fetch some big stones," said the mother goat. "While the wolf's still asleep, we'll fill his stomach with them."

The seven little kids dashed off and fetched the stones. They stuffed as many as they could into the wolf's stomach.

Then, quick as a flash, the mother goat sewed it
up again—so cleverly that he didn't feel a thing. He
never even twitched.

When he had slept long enough, the wolf yawned

and got up. The stones in his stomach were making him thirsty. He decided to go and have a drink.

As he moved off, the stones lurched and clashed together, and he cried out:

"How my stomach grunts and groans!
I ate six kids, but they feel like stones."

He came to a well and tried to drink. But the stones inside him were so heavy that he lost his balance, fell into the water and was drowned. The

seven little kids and their mother were watching it
all. They skipped and jumped; they sang at the top
of their voices:

"The wolf is dead! The wolf is dead!" And round
and round the well they danced for joy.

The
Musicians
of Bremen

There was once an old donkey who had carried sacks
for the miller for many a long year. But now he was
getting too weak-kneed to work, and he guessed that
his master would soon want to get rid of him. So
one day he ran away and trotted off towards
Bremen to find a job as a musician. For he liked the
sound of his own voice, and even dreamed of
accompanying himself on the lute.

He hadn't gone far when he came to an old dog lying by the path, panting as if he had been running for hours.

"What's the matter?" asked the donkey.

"I'm worn out," said the dog. "I'm too old for hunting, so my master said he would get rid of me. I've run away, but what's the use? How can I keep going?"

"Cheer up," said the donkey. "I'm going to Bremen to find a job as a musician. Why don't you come too as my drummer?"

"But I haven't got a drum," said the dog sadly.

"We can soon buy one in Bremen," said the donkey.

The dog thought that a brilliant idea. He had got his breath back by now, and eagerly set off with the donkey. They hadn't gone far when they came to an old cat sitting shivering by the path.

"What's the matter?" asked the donkey.

"Nobody wants me," sighed the cat. "I'm too old to chase mice, and my teeth are beginning to fall out. My mistress said she would get rid of me, so I ran away to save her the trouble. But it hasn't done me much good so far. Where shall I go now?"

"Cheer up," said the donkey. "Come along with us to Bremen. You can sing soprano, can't you? Well then, we'll make our fortune together."

The cat thought that a brilliant idea. The three trotted along till they came to a farm. On the gate a cock was crowing desperately, as if his life depended on it.

"You certainly can sing," said the donkey.
"What's it all about?"

"The farmer's wife has asked visitors to dinner
tomorrow, and I heard her say she'll make me into
chicken soup. So I'm making as much noise as I
can; it's my last chance."

"Cheer up," said the donkey. "Come along with us to Bremen. We can do with an extra voice. You can be our tenor – that's a better idea than being made into soup, isn't it?"

The cock thought it was a brilliant idea, and the four friends went on their way together.

Soon they came to a forest, and as it was getting dark, they began to look for a place to sleep. The donkey and the dog lay down under a tree, the cat curled up on a bough and the cock fluttered up to one of the highest branches. From this high perch he could see a light shining through a window. So he told his friends there must be a house a little further on.

The dog agreed. With luck he might find a bone or two; perhaps there would even be some meat left

on one of them. They all followed their noses and made straight for the lighted window.

They crept up to the house, but the donkey was the only one tall enough to see inside.

"What can you see?" asked the cock.

"Haw, haw, what can I see?" said the donkey. "A table with plenty to eat and drink—just what we want—and six robbers tucking in."

"Then there won't be anything left for us," said the cock.

"Oh yes, there will," said the donkey, "if we use our wits."

So they all tried hard to think of a way to turn the robbers out of the house and settle there themselves. At last they had a brilliant idea—they would sing for their supper. The donkey stood with his forefeet on the window-sill, the dog jumped on to his back, the cat climbed on top of the dog and the cock flew on to the cat's head.

When they were all ready, the donkey said: "SING!" They all sang fortissimo and frightened the robbers so much that they rushed off into the forest, sure that terrifying monsters were after them.

The four musicians felt that their plan had worked splendidly. They lost no time in getting to the table, finding their favourite food and gobbling as much as they could eat.

They soon felt very full and floppy, and looked round for somewhere to sleep. They put out the light, and the donkey lay down on some straw in the yard, the dog crouched in a corner behind the back door and the cat curled up on

the warm hearth. The cock flew up and perched on a high rafter. And they all fell fast asleep.

At one o'clock, at dead of night, the robbers came out from their hiding places and saw that the house was quite dark.

"It's all right, we can go back now," whispered
their leader. "We shouldn't have been scared off so
easily." But he did not feel as brave as he sounded,
so he sent one of the others back to make sure that
the house was empty.

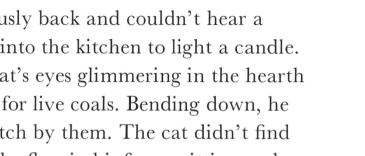

He crept cautiously back and couldn't hear a
sound, so he went into the kitchen to light a candle.
He could see the cat's eyes glimmering in the hearth
and mistook them for live coals. Bending down, he
tried to light a match by them. The cat didn't find
this at all funny. She flew in his face, spitting and
scratching.

The robber was terrified. He groped his way

to the back door, but before he reached it the dog jumped up and bit his leg. As he ran across the yard, the donkey gave him a sharp kick and the cock crowed with a piercing shriek from the rafter: "*Cockadoodle doo! Cockadoodle doo!*"

Rushing back to the others, the robber told them how he had been treated: "There's a wicked witch in the house—she spat at me and scratched my face with her long nails. And there's an armed man hiding behind the door—as I came out he stabbed me in the leg. In the yard there's a great hairy monster, who beat me with his club, and—worst of all—on the roof there's an old *judge;* when he saw me he yelled: '*Catch that crook! Catch that crook!*'"

By now the robbers were all quite sure that the house was no place for them, and they were soon miles away. But the four musicians settled in very

comfortably. They were in no hurry to go on to
Bremen. They all agreed that it would be silly to
leave a good home that suited them so well, and I
expect they are still there.

Puss in Boots

Once upon a time there was a miller who had three sons, his mill, his donkey and a cat. The miller's sons worked the mill, the donkey fetched corn to be ground and carried away the flour, and the cat caught mice. When the miller died, his three sons divided their inheritance. The eldest son got the mill, the second son got the donkey, and as there was nothing else left for him the third son got the cat. He was very downcast. "I have come off worst of all," he said to himself. "My eldest brother can work the mill, my second brother can ride his donkey, but what can I do with a cat? I'll have his skin made into a pair of fur gloves, and that will be that."

"Listen to me," said the cat, who had understood everything the young man said. "You don't want to kill me just to make my fur into gloves! Have a pair of boots made for me, so that I can get out and about and show myself in public, and your fortunes will soon be on the mend."

The miller's son was rather surprised to hear his cat talking like this, but since a cobbler happened to be passing by he called him in and told him to measure the cat for a pair of boots.

When the boots were made, the cat put them on, got a sack and put a little grain in it, fastened a string to the top so that he could close it by pulling the string, slung the sack over his shoulder and walked out of the mill, going on two legs like a man.

Now the King who ruled that country at the time was very fond of eating partridges, but sad to say, he could not get any. The forest was full of them, but they were so timid that no marksman could bring them down. The cat knew this, and he had thought of a way to start making his master's fortune. When he came to the forest he opened his sack, spreading out the grain inside it, and laid the string in the grass, leading the end of it to the other side of a hedge. He lay in wait behind the hedge himself.

Soon the partridges came along and found the grain. One by one, they hopped into the sack. When he had a good many inside his sack, the cat pulled the string at the top tight, to close it, slung it on his back, and marched off to the King's palace.

"Halt!" said the guard at the gate. "Where are you going?"

"I want to see the King," replied the cat.

"You must be crazy!" said the guard. "A cat, go to see the King?"

"Oh, let him in," said another man. "The King is often bored. Maybe this strange cat and his fancies will amuse him."

So the cat came before the King. He bowed very low and said, "My master the Count – " and here he added a very long, grand name – "sends Your Majesty his compliments and these partridges, which he has just caught in his snares."

The King was delighted, and admired the fine fat partridges. He ordered his servants to give the cat as much gold from his treasury as he could carry in his sack. "Take that to your master, and give him my hearty thanks for his present," said the King.

The poor miller's son was sitting by the window at home, his chin propped on his hand, thinking sadly that he had given the last of his money to pay for the cat's boots, and what good could the cat do him in return? Then in came the cat, dropped the sack on the floor, untied it and tipped the gold out in front of the miller's son.

"That's for you," said the cat, "and His Majesty sends you his compliments and hearty thanks."

The miller's son was delighted with his new riches, though he could hardly understand how he had come by them. However, the cat told him the whole story as he pulled off his boots.

"You have plenty of money now," he said, "but we shall do better still. Tomorrow I'll put on my boots again, and you will soon be even richer. And I have told the King you are a Count."

Next day the cat did as he had said: he put on his boots and went hunting again. He had a fine catch of partridges, and took them to the King. So it went on, day after day, and day after day the cat brought more gold home. He became such a favourite of the King's that he was allowed to go in and out and walk around the palace, just as he liked.

One day the cat was standing by the fire in the King's kitchens, warming himself, when in came the King's coachman, grumbling.

"I wish the King and Princess would go to the devil!" said he. "I was just off to the tavern for a drink and a game of cards, and now I'm told to take them driving down to the lake."

On hearing this, the cat slipped away and hurried home. He said to his master, "If you want to be a Count and grow rich, come with me and go swimming in the lake!"

The young miller did not know what to make of that, but he did as the

cat told him, went down to the lake, stripped off his clothes and jumped into the water.

However, the cat picked up his master's clothes, carried them away and hid them. No sooner had he done so than the King came driving by. The cat immediately began to wail most piteously. "Oh, Your Majesty! My master was swimming here in the lake, when a thief came along and stole his clothes from the bank where they were lying. Now my master the Count is in the water and can't come out! If he stays there much longer he will catch his death of cold!"

When the King heard the cat's story, he ordered the coachman to wait, and one of the courtiers was told to ride back and fetch some of the King's own clothes. The Count, as he must now be called, put on these magnificent garments, and as the King felt much obliged to him for the partridges anyway, thinking it was the Count who had sent them, he invited the young man to get into the royal coach. The Princess had no objection, since the Count was young and handsome, and she liked him very well indeed.

Meanwhile, the cat had gone on ahead. He came to a great meadow, where over a hundred men were making hay.

"Who owns this meadow, good people?" asked the cat.

"It belongs to the great enchanter."

"Now listen to me! The King will soon come driving by, and when he asks who owns this meadow you must say: The Count. And if you don't, you will all be killed stone dead."

So the cat went on, and came to a cornfield so wide you could not see from one side of it to the other, and there were over two hundred men there cutting the corn.

"Who owns this corn, good people?"

"It belongs to the enchanter."

"Now listen to me! The King will soon come driving by, and when he asks who owns this corn you must say: The Count. And if you don't, you will all be killed stone dead."

Last of all the cat came to a vast forest, and there were over three hundred men there felling the great oak trees and chopping them up.

"Who owns this forest, good people?"

"It belongs to the enchanter."

"Now listen to me! The King will soon come driving by, and when he asks who owns this forest you must say: The Count. And if you don't, you will all be killed stone dead."

The cat walked on. Everyone stared after him, and because he looked so strange, walking on his hind legs like a man and wearing a pair of boots, the people were all afraid of him.

Soon he came to the enchanter's castle and marched boldly in. The enchanter looked disdainfully at him, and asked what he wanted.

The cat bowed very low. "I have heard tell that you can turn yourself into any animal you like," he said. "Well, I dare say you can turn yourself into a dog or a fox or a wolf, but I shouldn't think you could turn into a great animal like an elephant, so I came to find out for myself.''

"Oh, that's child's play to me!" said the enchanter, and next moment he had turned himself into an elephant.

"Remarkable," said the cat. "But can you turn into a lion?"

"That's easy too," said the enchanter, and there he stood in front of the cat, in the shape of a lion.

The cat pretended to be terrified. "Amazing!" he cried. "Incredible!

Never in my wildest dreams would I have thought such a thing possible! Of course, it would be even more amazing if you could turn into something as small as a mouse. I'm sure you can work more magic than any other enchanter in the world, but I can't help thinking that would be beyond you."

Flattered by the cat's compliments, the enchanter said, "Oh no, my dear Cat, I can do that too!" And next moment he was a mouse scampering round the room. In a moment the cat was after it, and with one bound he leaped on the mouse and ate it all up.

Meanwhile, the King, the Count and the Princess had been driving on, and they came to the great meadow. "Who owns this hay?" asked the King.

"Our master the Count," said all the men, just as the cat had told them.

"This is a fine piece of land, Count," said the King.

After that they came to the wide cornfield. "Who owns this corn, good people?" asked the King.

"Our master the Count."

"Why, my dear Count, you have very fine estates!" said the King.

Then they came to the forest. "Who owns these trees, good people?" asked the King.

"Our master the Count."

The King was more impressed than ever. "You must be a rich man, Count," said he. "I don't believe I have so magnificent a forest on my own estates."

At last they came to the castle. The cat was standing at the top of the stairs, and when the coach drew up outside he ran downstairs and opened the doors. "Your Majesty," he said, "this is the castle of my master the Count, who will remember the honour of your visit with gratitude to his dying day."

The King stepped out of the coach, and admired the magnificent building, which was almost larger and finer than his own royal palace. As for the Count, he led the Princess upstairs to the great hall, which sparkled with gold and jewels.

Then the Princess was betrothed to the Count, and when the King died the Count became king himself, and Puss in Boots was his Prime Minister.

Tom Thumb

Once upon a time there was a poor countryman, and he was sitting by his fireside one evening poking the fire, while his wife sat and span. "How sad I am that we have no children!" said he. "This place is so quiet, and other people's houses are all so lively and merry!"

"Yes," said his wife, sighing, "if only we had a child, just one, however small, even a child no bigger than my thumb, then I'd be happy, and we would love it dearly!"

Well, seven months later it so happened that she did have a child, a little boy who was perfectly formed in every way, but no bigger than a man's thumb.

So the countryman and his wife said, "Well, we have what we wanted, and he is our own dear child." And because the boy was so small, they called him Tom Thumb.

They gave him plenty to eat, but he never grew any bigger; he stayed as small as the day he was born. However, he had a pair of quick bright eyes. Soon he proved to be a clever, nimble boy, and whatever he set out to do, he did it well.

One day his father was going off to the forest to chop some wood, and he said, half to himself, "I wish I had someone to follow me with the cart."

"Oh, don't you worry, Father," said Tom Thumb. "I'll bring the cart to the forest for you whenever you need it."

That made his father laugh. "How could you do that?" he asked. "You're far too small to drive a horse and cart!"

"Never mind that, Father. If Mother will harness up the horse, I'll sit in his ear and tell him which way to go."

"Very well," said his father. "There's no harm in trying."

So when the time came, Tom Thumb's mother harnessed up the horse, lifted Tom Thumb up, and he sat in the horse's ear and called out which way they were to go. "Gee up!" he shouted. All went well; Tom Thumb might have been driving a horse and cart all his life, and they took the right path to the forest. But just as the cart was turning a corner, and Tom Thumb was calling, "Whoa there!" two strangers came by.

"Good Heavens!" said one of them. "Whatever is that? I can see a cart going along the road, and I can hear a driver calling out to the horse, yet there isn't any driver to be seen!"

"There's something funny about it, sure enough," agreed the other man. "Let's follow and see where the cart is going."

The cart went on, right into the forest, to the place where Tom Thumb's father was chopping wood. When Tom Thumb saw his father, he called out, "You see, Father? Here I am, and here's the cart too! Lift me down now."

His father held the horse with his left hand, took Tom Thumb out of the horse's ear with his right hand, and Tom Thumb sat down on a blade of grass, very pleased with himself.

When the two strangers caught sight of Tom Thumb, they were so surprised, they could not speak. But then one of them drew the other aside. "Listen, that little fellow might make our fortunes!" said he. "We could put him on show in some big city, and make people pay to see him. Let's buy him!"

So they went up to Tom Thumb's father and said, "Will you sell us that little fellow? We'll take good care of him."

"Oh, no," said the father. "I can't do that; he's the apple of my eye, and I wouldn't part with him for all the gold in the world!"

However, when Tom Thumb heard this bargaining, he climbed the folds of his father's coat, got up on his shoulder, and whispered in his ear, "Go on, Father, sell me! I'll soon come home again." So his father sold him to the two strangers for a great deal of money.

"Now, where would you like to sit?" asked one of the men.

"Oh, just put me on the brim of your hat," said Tom Thumb. "I can walk up and down there and look at the view. I won't fall off."

So they did as he asked, and when Tom Thumb had said goodbye to his father they all three set off together.

On they went, till twilight began to fall, and the little boy said, "Put me down, please. It's urgent!"

"No, you just stay where you are," said the man on whose head he was standing. "Nothing you do will bother me; I've had bird droppings on this hat before now!"

"No, no!" said Tom Thumb. "I know what's right and proper. Quick, do put me down!"

So the man took off his hat and put the little boy down in a field by the wayside. Tom Thumb scurried about among the clods of earth for a moment or so, and then, spotting a mousehole, he crawled inside it.

"Goodbye, gentlemen!" said he. "You can go off home without me!"

And he laughed and laughed. They came and poked sticks down the mousehole, and that did them no good; Tom Thumb just crept further in, and as it was soon quite dark they had to go home empty-handed, in a very bad temper.

When Tom Thumb was sure they had gone, he crept out of the mousehole again. "Crossing a field like this in the dark is dangerous," he thought. "I could easily break a leg, or my neck." But luckily he came upon an empty snail-shell. "That's a good thing!" he said. "I can spend the night quite safely here." And he went inside.

Quite soon, just as he was dropping off to sleep, he heard two men walking by.

"Now," one of them was saying to the other, "how shall we set about stealing that rich minister's money and his silver?"

Tom Thumb spoke up. "I can tell you how!" said he.

"What was that?" asked the thief, in alarm. "I'm sure I heard a voice!"

They stopped and listened, and Tom Thumb spoke up again. "Take me with you, and I'll help you."

"But where are you?"

"Just look down on the ground here, and you'll find where my voice is coming from," said Tom Thumb.

So at last the thieves found him and picked him up. "Well, little fellow, and how can you help us?" they asked.

"Why," said Tom Thumb, "I can creep through the iron bars across the window of the minister's room and hand you out the things you want."

"Very well," they said, "let's try it!"

When they came to the house, Tom Thumb crept into the minister's room, but once inside he shouted at the top of his voice, "Do you want everything that's here?"

The thieves were scared. "Hush!" they said. "Keep your voice down, or you'll wake the household!"

But Tom Thumb pretended not to understand them, and he shouted out again, "What do you want? Do you want everything that's here?"

Now the maidservant sleeping in the next room heard him, and she sat up in bed and listened. The thieves had run a little way off in their fright, but at last they plucked up courage again. "The little fellow's only teasing us," they thought, so they came back and whispered, "Come along, now, no more joking! Just pass the stuff out!"

Then Tom Thumb shouted again, as loud as ever he could: "Here, just put your hands in through the bars, and you can have it all!"

The maidservant, who was listening, heard him quite clearly, and she jumped out of bed and stumbled in through the door. The thieves ran away; they ran and ran as if the Devil himself were after them. Since the maidservant could not see anything, she went to fetch a light, and when she came back Tom Thumb managed to get out of the house without being noticed, and into the barn. As for the maidservant, when she had searched the whole room and still found nothing, at last she went back to bed, thinking she must have been dreaming with her eyes open.

Tom Thumb climbed into a heap of hay and found a good place to sleep; he decided to spend the night there and then go home to his parents. But there were more adventures in store for him!

When day dawned, the maidservant got up to go and feed the animals. The first place she went to was the barn, where she picked up an armful of hay, and it happened to be the hay where Tom Thumb was sleeping. Indeed, he was so fast asleep that he never noticed anything, and he didn't wake up until he was right inside the cow's mouth, along with some of the hay.

"Dear me!" he cried. "However did I get into this mill?" Soon, however, he realized where he was. He had to be very careful to avoid the cow's teeth, which might have chewed him up any moment, and then down he slid into her stomach.

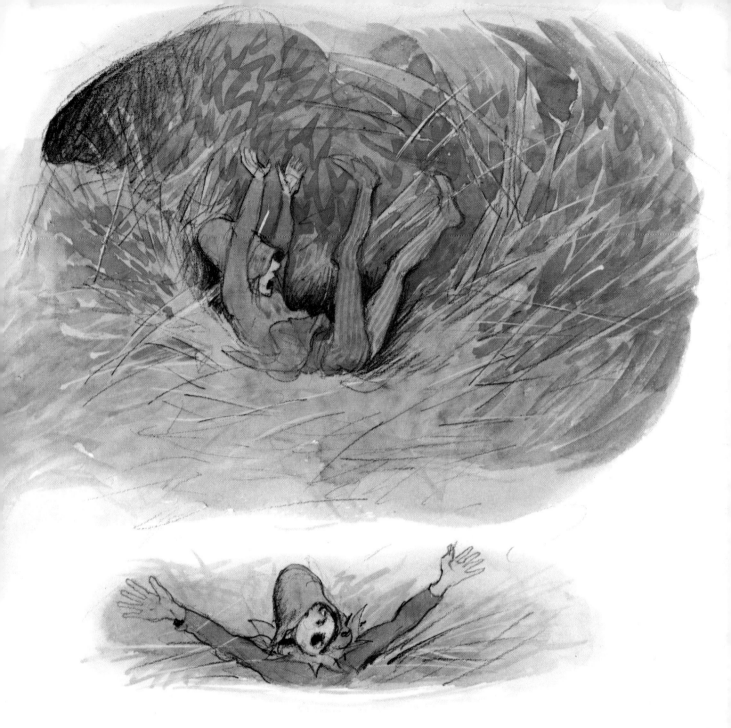

"They forgot the windows when they built this room," said he. "The sun can't shine in, and there isn't any lamp either!" He didn't like the place at all, and even worse, more and more hay kept coming in at the door, so that soon there was hardly any space left. At last he felt so frightened that he called out, as loud as he could, "No more hay, please! No more hay, please!"

The maidservant was just milking the cow when she heard someone speak, though she could not see him, and it was the very same voice she had heard the night before.

She was so frightened that she tumbled off her stool and spilled the bucket of milk. Off she ran to her master, as fast as she could go.

"Oh, sir!" she cried. "Our cow is talking!"

"Nonsense! You must be out of your mind!" said the minister. However, he went off to the cowshed himself to see what was going on.

No sooner did he set foot inside the shed than Tom Thumb started shouting again. "No more hay, please! No more hay, please!"

This frightened the minister, too. He thought his cow must be possessed by some evil demon, and he gave orders for her to be killed. So the cow was slaughtered, and her stomach, with Tom Thumb still inside it, was thrown on the dung heap. Tom Thumb had a hard job of it working his way out, but at last he made enough room to struggle free. However, just as he was about to pop his head out . . .

. . . he had another piece of bad luck. A hungry wolf came prowling by and swallowed the cow's stomach whole, in a single gulp. But Tom Thumb did not lose heart. "Perhaps this wolf will listen to me," he thought, and he called out from inside the wolf, "Dear Mr. Wolf, I can tell you where to find delicious things to eat!"

"Can you, indeed?" asked the wolf. "Where?"

"In a house I know. You must get in through the drain in the wall, and then you'll see all the cakes and bacon and sausages you can eat." And Tom Thumb told the wolf the way to his father's house.

The wolf wasn't wasting any time. That very night he got into the larder through the drain, and ate as much as he wanted. When he had had enough, he tried to get out again, but by now he was so fat that he could not leave the same way as he had come. That was what Tom Thumb had been hoping for, and now he began making a lot of noise inside the wolf, shouting and yelling at the top of his voice.

"Be quiet, can't you?" said the wolf. "You'll wake the household!"

"What if I do?" said Tom Thumb. "You've had your feast, now it's my turn for a bit of fun!"

And he began shouting at the top of his voice again.

At last the noise woke his father and mother. They came running to the larder and looked in through a crack in the door. When they saw a wolf inside they hurried off — his father to get his axe and his mother to fetch the scythe.

"Now, you stand back," said the man to his wife, as they came back to the larder. "I shall hit him with the axe, and if that doesn't kill him then you must cut his body open."

Tom Thumb, hearing his father's voice, called out, "Here I am, Father! I'm inside the wolf!"

"Thank heavens!" cried his father joyfully. "Our own dear child is home again!"

And he told his wife to put down the scythe for fear of hurting Tom Thumb. Then he swung his axe, and gave the wolf such a mighty blow that he fell down dead. Tom Thumb's mother and father fetched a knife and a pair of scissors, cut open the wolf's body and found their little boy.

"Dear me, we've been so worried about you!" said his father.

"Oh, Father, I've had so many adventures! How glad I am to breathe fresh air again!"

"But where have you been all this time?"

"I've been down a mousehole, Father, in the stomach of a cow, and in the wolf's belly, and now I'm back home!"

"And we'll never sell you again, not for all the money in the world!" said his parents, hugging and kissing their own dear little Tom Thumb. They gave him something to eat and something to drink, and they had new clothes made for him, because his old ones were ruined after all his adventures.